For Mom and Dad, who helped me think big. —L. G. S.

Thank you, Ha-Shem, for lending me your genius.
For my children, Zoe, Ben, Chyna, Issy, Chris, and Eli,
think even bigger, guys! —V. B. N.

Text copyright © 2012 by Liz Garton Scanlon
Illustrations copyright © 2012 by Vanessa Brantley Newton

First published in the United States of America in July 2012
by Bloomsbury Books for Young Readers
www.bloomsburykids.com

For information about permission to reproduce selections from this book, write to
Permissions, Bloomsbury BFYR, 175 Fifth Avenue, New York, New York 10010

Library of Congress Cataloging-in-Publication Data
Scanlon, Elizabeth Garton.
Think big / by Liz Garton Scanlon ; illustrated by Vanessa Brantley Newton. — 1st U.S. ed.
p.   cm.
Summary: A classroom of exuberant youngsters explores art in its most varied forms,
from painting, music, and writing to cooking and performing.
ISBN 978-1-59990-611-9 (hardcover) • ISBN 978-1-59990-612-6 (reinforced)
[1. Stories in rhyme. 2. Arts—Fiction. 3. Creative ability—Fiction.]
I. Newton, Vanessa Brantley, ill. II. Title.
PZ8.3.S2798Th 2012   [E]—dc23   2011035102

The art is a digital collage of gouache, charcoal, and mixed media
Typeset in Elroy
Book design by Donna Mark

Printed in China by Hung Hing Printing (China) Co., Ltd., Shenzhen, Guangdong
(hardcover) 10 9 8 7 6 5 4 3 2 1
(reinforced) 10 9 8 7 6 5 4 3 2 1

When I Grow up!!!

Think Big

Liz Garton Scanlon

illustrated by

Vanessa Brantley Newton

BLOOMSBURY

NEW YORK BERLIN LONDON SYDNEY

Thick paint

Deep hue

Bow stroke

One, two

Brainstorm
Blank page

Scene set
Onstage

Pinch salt

Dice, chop

Click, flash

Time stop

Big voice
On pitch

Pin, trim
Thread, stitch

Red clay

Round wheel

Spin, twirl

Toe, heel

Black ink

Line, shade

Knit, purl

No thought

Too great

You think

We'll wait

Imagine

Big breath

Brave heart

Ready, set . . .

Make art!

reserting
hen we grow-up!